THE BLACK DIAMOND
DETECTIVE AGENCY

THE BLACK DIAMOND DETECTIVE AGENCY

—Containing—

MAYHEM, MYSTERY, ROMANCE, MINE SHAFTS, BULLETS.

FRAMED AS A GRAPHICAL NARRATIVE

BY MR. EDDIE CAMPBELL

INSPIRED BY THE SCREENPLAY OF

MR. C. GABY MITCHELL

UNDER THE AUSPICES OF
THE ILLUSTRIOUS

WILLIAM HORBERG, ESQ.

:01
FIRST SECOND
New York & London.

Fine picture novels since '06.

And you mean to spend the rest of your life hiding behind fake glasses?

We need to move on, Jackie.
It's been two years.
Dear Frank.
Dear Frank.
she's not coming back.

September 3, 1899

The night before the day it all went wrong.

Part 1:
FRAMES

The day it all went wrong
started out fine.

Through his new glasses,
the trees are a lush green; the corn is ripe.

He can see the red-headed woodpecker that is—

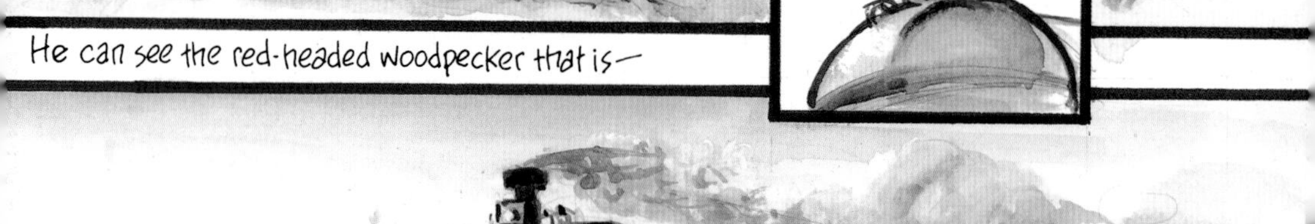

The morning train is bang on time.

The people are all out waiting.
TOPEL
LEBANON
LEBANON MO.
WHO NEEDS WHO?
The puzzled engineer and fireman lean out of the engine house.
Sam Connors looks uncomfortable. He waves.
AND THE TRAIN IS BANG ON TIME.

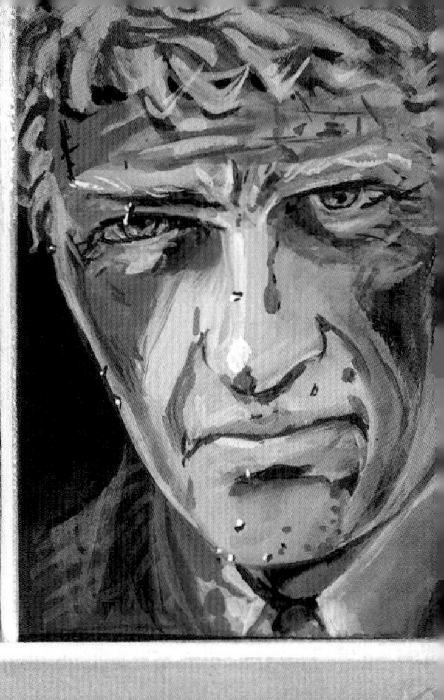

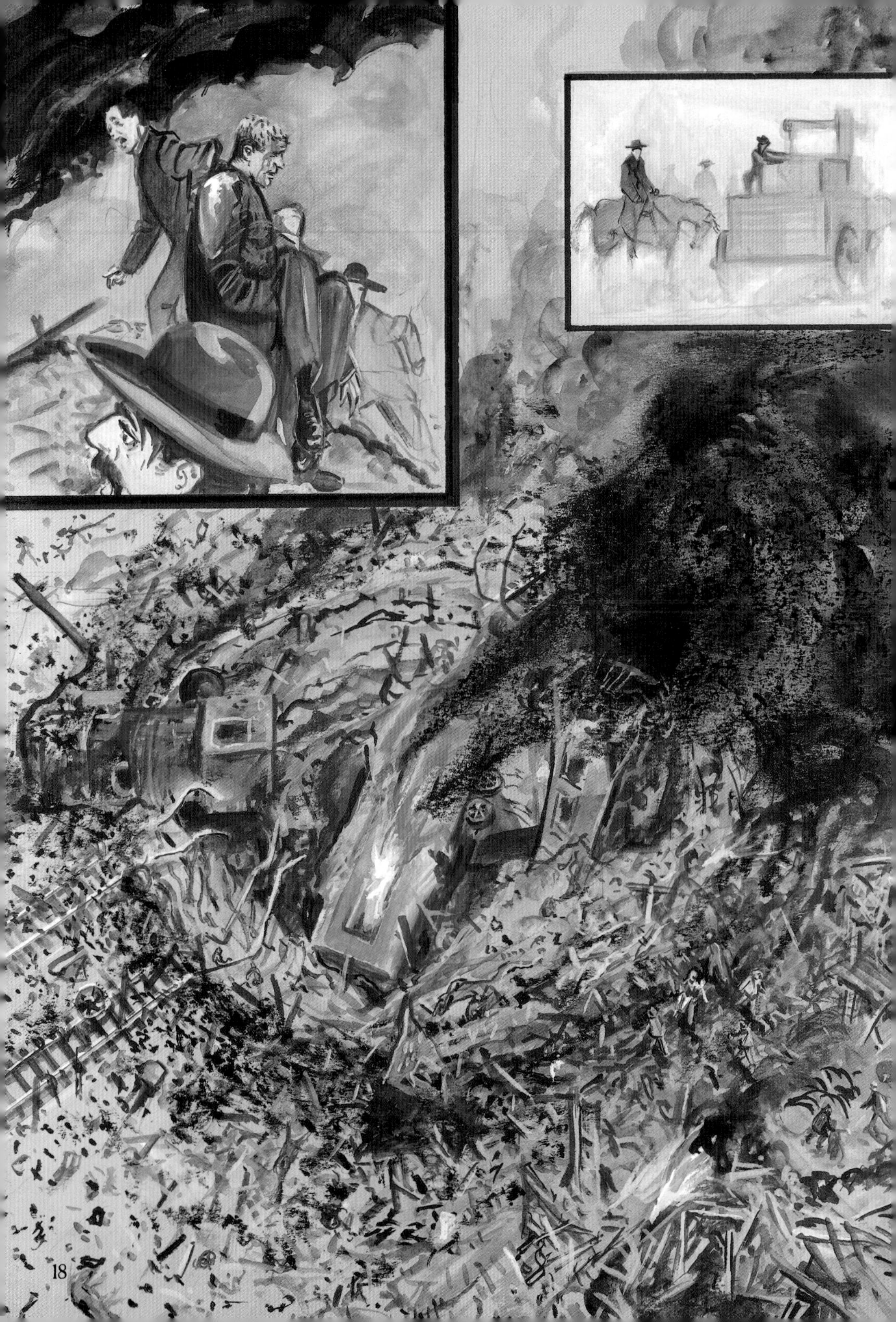

Dear Jackie

HOTEL

against who you are but I beg you
do not follow me, Jackie
Please don't —
Julie.

Dear

CORRINE
HARDIN
1894-1897

SIMMS
BLACK
DIAMOND
DETECTIVE
AGENCY

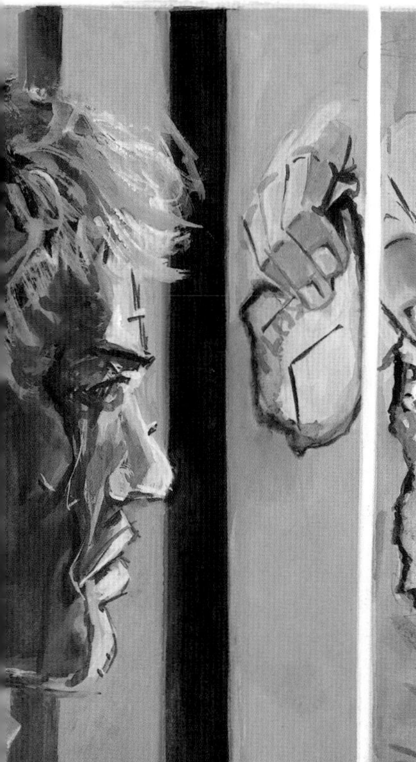

PLOSIVES
DRYES EXPLOSIVES,
CHICAGO ILLINOIS
Nitrogl
John Hardin
Lebanon
Missour

GO ILLIN
tro
John Hardin
Lebano
Missour

Hear me Now, Hardin? Let's start over then. I'm Detective Larkin; my colleague is Mr. Simms. You are neck-deep in shit. What do you know?

Town meeting yesterday morning about new freight rates for corn. Too high. Nobody could pay. They must have got carried away and put up a barricade to stop the train. I was late.

What did you see?
Came to...everything gone. Big box. maybe a safe. picked up.
WHO picked it up?

Faces covered. Smoke. I couldn't-

The people we talked to said you and your wife showed up out of nowhere 4/5 years ago. Kept to yourself.

Where'd you come from? Who helped you pull this off? Where's your wife? Hid out? Waiting?

If I was blowing up half the town, why would I hang around?
THAT'S a good question, Mr. Hardin. Lessee... perhaps you walked out without your wallet... so... you rush back, then—
BA BOOM!
your names on the goddamn nitro boxes.
The goddamn boxes.
Where did you come here from, Hardin? Hmm?
Why would you need to think about that?
Do you know who we are? We're private detectives. Which means we can go into any town... in any state. Soon we'll know more about you than you seem to know about yourself.
We'll find out what happened here. In a few hours there'll be more Black Diamond detectives and government agents here than—
YOU WITH me, Hardin?

Go home!
Leave this to the Law.

DAMN DOOR!... You know what, Hardin? A guilty man needs to talk.
It's just the gettin' start—

oh.

Very bad feelin' in the air. Everybody's hurt..and angry too. We're gonna need reinforcements by mornin'.

Crowd outside the jail's gettin' downright scary.

=gnh=

Hey, Billy, here's the- oh goddamn it!!

I told you. Just leaning the bars in front of the cell wasn't going to hold him.
Can you see my eyeglasses?

Uh... no.
Then the bastard took them!

He stole yer goddamn glasses? That means it's me who's gotta finish the report.
Everything's broke, Bob.

It's a sign of the times, Billy.
No point in asking if he took your gun too.

But how did he get out? Nobody used the front door.
Oh yeah: the roof.
Y'know, that telegraph pole doesn't go with the curtains.

Mr. Quindlin!
How'd you two get here so fast?
We were in Kansas City investigating those bank robberies when —
This Hardin: Secret Service do a drawing of h—?
Yes, sir.
Oh Christ.
Ed, make sure we map and number everything for Dr. Lefarge.
Yes sir.
Put four men on the trail of the wagon and four more on Hardin.
I woulda went for the son of a bitch, sir, but we thought we—
No one wants to see you get shot with your own gun, Billy.

Here comes the Secret Service.
ssh
Ah! Chief Lambert.
Mr. Quindlin.
We'll cover the roads.
YOU'LL cover-! I guess everything's all right, then.
Now, now... It wasn't just Secret Service agents on the train. Four of my best-
Your best! LOOK! This is what security looks like when it's diluted by an outside organization!
I beg your pardon, Mr. Lambert. The Secret Service asked us to participate.
Oh, we'll be askin' you a lot of things. Such as how the Bomber hikes up his trousers and walks out of jail right in front of you.
SHERIFF

Mr. Lambert, none of us know what was in the safe. And we NEED to know.
That's classified information.
Well, unclassify it. It's gone.
Let me remind you, Mr. Quindlin, that you were brought along on this because you have a contract with the railroad, and that it was a top secret trip which had its security breached specifically by the inclusion of your agency.
WHA-?
The bomber knew the route and-
WE didn't know the route even though I made requests for it.
It was class-i-fied.
So we couldn't leak information we DIDN'T HAVE.

What about tracks, detective? A load as heavy as this one's supposed to be, the ruts would be deep.

Rain washed most of 'em out.

They had to stay on a road. Can't go just anywhere with something that size.

If they didn't get where they were headed before the rains, they'll be mired up to their axles in mud. Which means they can't be far. Either on purpose, or stuck.

We're better off hunting together.

HARDWARE
These must be our boys, then. Open 'em up for the men, Ed.
Sir?
And keep Carl away.
We got enough men to STOP him?
Carl. stay here; that's an order.
Carl!

Dr LeFARGE

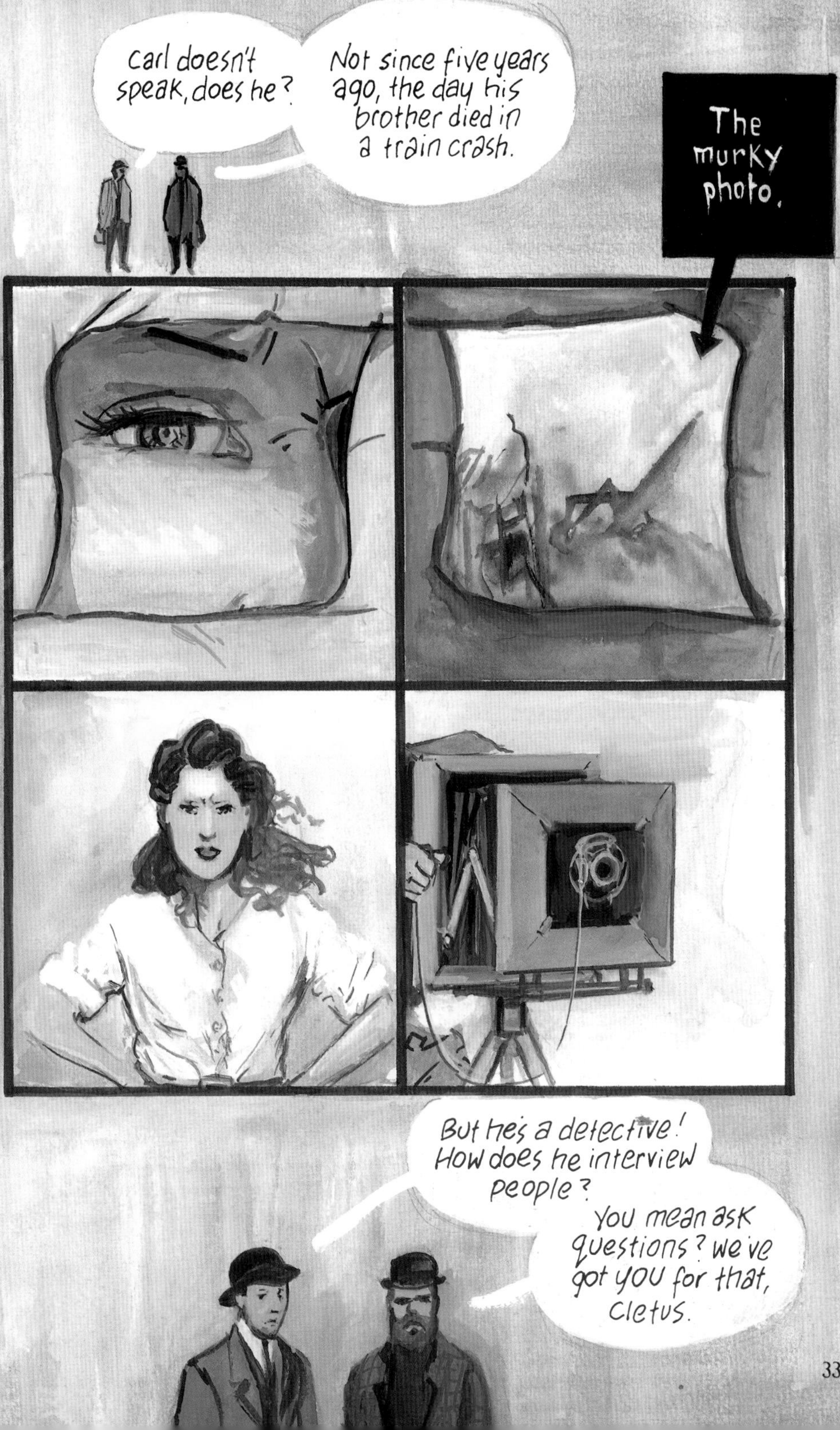

Carl doesn't speak, does he?
Not since five years ago, the day his brother died in a train crash.
The murky photo.

But he's a detective! How does he interview people?
You mean ask questions? We've got YOU for that, Cletus.

Dear Jack
Do not follow.
WANTED
Lebanon bombing
$5,000 ALIVE
The crap poster

Mr. Phillips, we've got the place sealed tight as a drum. It looks like they drove into the big mine, but there's no sign they ever came out again.
DANG
Must be miles down! If the wagon's in here, it's gone.

TEN YEAR OLD

The dear Frank letter

These men were our friends and brothers. Finding their killers won't bring them back or make us feel better. But we'll honor them by doing our jobs as they would for us if we were in their place.
This is what we have: A man claiming to be a farmer, from a town up the line, came here the night before the bombing and got some of the farmers riled up against the railroad. He turned what was supposed to be a simple town meeting the next morning about crop shipping prices into a train stopping barricade. I have a hunch that we'll find this man with the bombers.
Doctor LeFarge.
The nitroglycerine was not on the train. It was buried beneath the tracks. Why the train was blown up in town when there are hundreds of miles of empty rails on both sides of it, I have no clue.

The safe, and whatever was in it, was taken from the train. We tracked it to a disused mineshaft where it had been disposed of along with the wagon and horses and probably a good number of thieves as well.
And then we've got the nitro box labels with this man Hardin's name on them.
We turned over Hardin's place and found that 'Dear Frank' letter in the trash.
Dear Frank
A woman at the store said Hardin's wife bought postage for a letter to Chicago four or five months ago.
And the box labels are from a Chicago manufacturer by the name of Dryer.
Maybe Chicago is a break. If this Hardin is from there, ever been there or thought about going- I want to know. I WANT to know who was working WITH him. I want to know what happened to his WIFE, and I want to know who the HELL 'Dear Frank,' is, and I don't want anybody to eat a full meal or sleep the night through until I DO know it.
AT NORTHSP
EMPIRE
1914

MADISON St
449

Open up, Mrs. Sumner!

She here?
No.
When did you hear from her last?
The day she left with you.
She wrote you.
No.
I saw her.
She was always writing letters she never mailed. Even wrote to the dead.
She was a little crazy, you know.
Where'd you go?
Away. We had a child. Julie named her Corrine.
After me?
She was the light of the world.
Was?

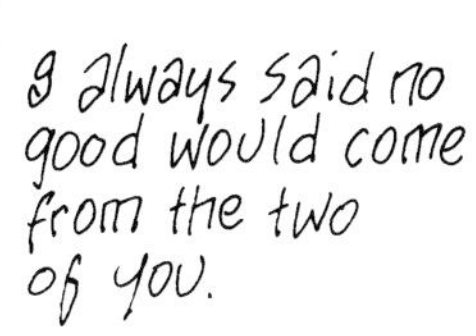

ST MARY'S ASYLUM ORPHANAGE

Sadie, how's it looking?

They're all as murky as that one, Mark.
Go in close and there isn't a single recognizable object.
Stand far enough back and it might as well be the lives of insects.
How do you get something so awful into a picture?
Speaking of pictures; Quindlin wants to see you.

Pulled in 43 sighting reports from the paper. All bogus. I'm just saying maybe the poster's crap.
Larkin and Simms saw him. What did THEY say about the likeness?
They said he was so cut up and bloody they couldn't tell WHAT he looked like.
The Chicago
OCTOBER 15 1899
LEBA
GRIEF
you asked for me, Mr. Quindlin?
Sadie, we need a better picture of the bomber.
you said I wouldn't have to do any more drawings. you promised.
You were there. You saw.
Go to Lebanon, and bring back his face. Please, Sadie.
Go with her, Mark. Talk to everyone again. Now the shock's worn off, maybe they'll remember more.

J.S DRYER EXPLOSI
KEEP OUT
DRYER EXPLO
MANUFACTU
!
Easy, now. I'm brittle.
You sold a load of nitroglycerine to a John Hardin.
I've been all over this with the detectives and the Government boys.
Who are YOU?

nice.

What did Hardin look like?

Couldn't say.

You gave him a load of nitro without looking at him?

Son, you have to have a work order from a mining operation or a company that specializes in... if you don't know how to move this stuff you could blow your dress up just driving it out the gate.

Hardin knew how?

He did and he had a work order.

Let's see it.

Papers were stole from the office.

Did he look like me?

He was taller. Fancy suit, hat pulled down so it bent his ears, and as big a wad of money as I've ever seen, which is probably why I can't recall his face.

And you're sure it was him, ma'am?
Oh, I felt him before I saw him. It was a cold hand of death.
It ran all the way down me. Then he walked by.
He walked by THAT window?
Yes.
Did he stoop and look in?
God forbid.
Well then, was he on his damned KNEES, ma'am?

See the powder? nothing.
so?
watch!
puff!
Look. Turns green. This piece of wood is from the train cars. The powder reacts to the traces of nitroglycerine on it.
The box end was nowhere near the explosion.
Doctor LeFarge, are you telling me it was put there afterwards?
That's the one logical conclusion, Mr. Quindlin.
And since Hardin's name is on the box label we should consider it a possibility that he's being framed.

LARKIN
Dear Jack
Do not

JEWELRY
CLOCKS WATCHES
LOANS
KEEP

Sit on it, Weasel, you're making me queasy.
who the fuck-?
I said who the fuck are you, mister?
Take your hand out from under the pillow!
Weasel- how does Frank get his mail?
Fra—
Fuck me!
Jackie.
But you're dead.

You were Frank's boy. You're still Frank's boy. That's why you're alive.
He can't be using his real name, but he musta got a letter or somethin' with his real name on it 'cause-
I find out you know where he is—
I don't, an' if he's alive, don't tell him where I am neither.
odd...I didn't see ANYONE I know on the street.
It's a hard fuckin' life, ain't it!

Was it money on the train, is that...?
I don't know, ma'am.
What was it about his eyes again?

They were like my father's after the war. Sad, far away. He said he'd seen too many things with them and guessed they'd never be right.

one bang and the cemetery population doubles.

Anything physical about him; birthmarks, scars, anything like that, Doctor?
He was badly hurt, wouldn't let me sew him up, kept carrying people in.

carrying 'em IN?
He SAVED a lot of lives that day.
I know, I know.

POST OFFICE

PURITY GUARANTEED
TEN YEAR OLD

General delivery for Frank Reno?
$10,000 Alive
Mr Reno? Frank Reno?
Mr. Frank for collection
Frank.- Jackie is back - Weasel.

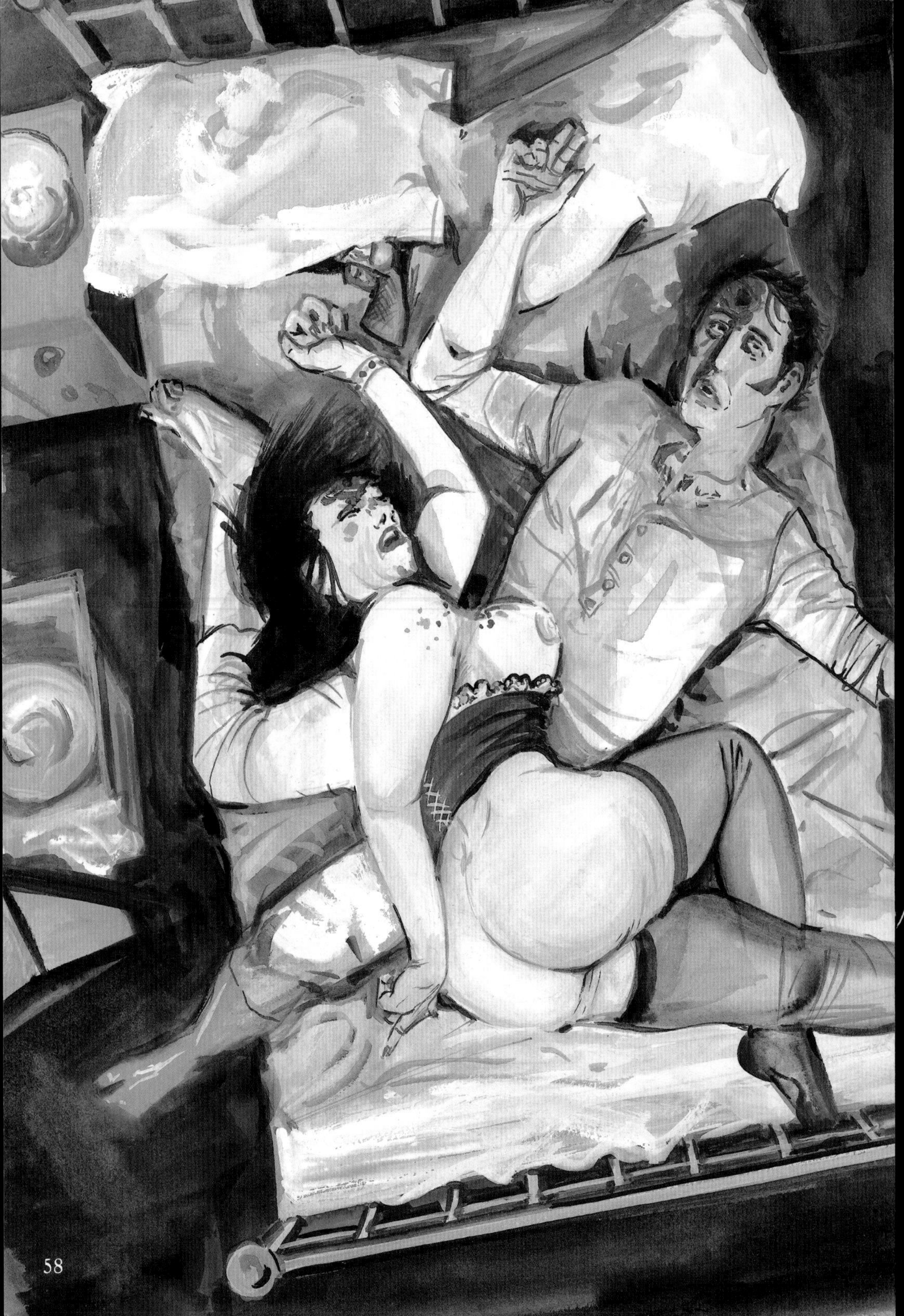

They're one step ahead of me. They know I made contact with Weasel even though I intercepted his message to Frank. And now they've cancelled Weasel's ticket..

On the job, heh? Anything I can do?
No thanks.

Would you mind putting it up somewhere for us, please?
It's really not something you want the guests to see.
It's no John Singer Sargent, but I wouldn't ask if it wasn't important.
WANTED
If there's ever a problem around here I can help you with... Ed Howell's the name.
I appreciate it. By the way, did you find the lady?
pardon?
One of your detectives came looking for a lady in a watch.

I don't know about Art, but that poster's about as use-ful as a dog-turd.
HA!
The Yellow Kid guy's got nothing on you, Carl. Maybe you shoulda drawn the poster.
Woman in a goddamn watch!

Christ, Sadie.

Part 2: Secrets

FREE
PUBLIC BATH No 3
Black Di
Agency, Ch
Hiring now
pply i
Fill this out and someone will see you.
BLACK DIAMOND

No.1
TED
JOHN HARDIN
LEBANON BOMBER
$10,000 REWARD
No.2
WANTED
DWIGHT EMERSON
TRAIN ROBBERY-MURDER
$2,000 REWARD
TED
No.5
WANTED
JAMES
ROB
No.6
WANTED
New picture
of bomber

I have to tell you, Mr....Collins, without a military record or police experience, your chances of being a detective are awfully slim.
My chances be better if I knew HIM?
No. 1
WANTED
Yeah, IF!
Mr. Quindlin?
This man claims he knows the bomber.

Mr. Collins? are you all right?
The Photographs- A clever effect.
Claims he knows the bomber.
His name is Harte.
Jackie Harte.
How do you-?
They blew me up once.
Jackie Harte? Of the 12th Street gang?
yeah.
Can't be. I was a cop when Harte and the Reno brothers, the whole goddamn gang, was wiped out in an explosion at their bar eight years ago.
were you in the gang?
yeah.
We dug something like sixteen corpses outta that place.

When I got there that night the bar was locked up, which it'd never been before.
I went in through a back window.
They were all shot BEFORE the explosion. First I thought it may be another gang, or the cops-
cops!? you got to be-
Nobody got out?
Jackie and the Renos weren't there. 'Course I didn't stick around-

I was crawling back through the window when the place blew. I hit a wall across the alley.
Ed, I want everything we have on the 12th Street gang. I want PICTURES!
Never got any, Not of the Renos or Harte.
'cause they had half the police force in their pocket.
BULL-
-SHIT!

Jeezus!
We're back in Lebanon, Billy.
Mr. Simms and Mr. Larkin, meet Mr. Collins. He claims he knows the bomber.
So where do we find Harte?
I don't know what you got on Jackie, but he wasn't a powder man. Elias Reno woulda made the bomb; Frank woulda set it off.
FRANK!? "Dear Goddam Frank!"
Would you excuse us for just a minute, Mr. Collins? We'll get you a cup of coffee— whatever you like.

You're sure John Hardin is this Jackie Harte?
It's his face.
How well do you know him? Funny, we questioned him and I had a gut feeling he really didn't know anything.
Bullfuckingfrogshit! The guy's name's on the goddamn nitro boxes. He jumped jail...
made assholes of both of us, and now we find he's some gangster but he doesn't know anything. Simms, you're the stubbornest-
- SHUT UP, BILLY! Mr. Collins... Mr. Quindlin will talk to you in his office.

I want you to work with us. I want to see every piece of evidence we have through YOUR EYES.
What do you want?
To settle up.
You think Harte and the Renos killed their own people?
I never figured Jackie for it, but the Renos, yeah.
We're going to do this my way, do you understand? You'll be just another detective working for us. I don't want Secret Service getting its hands on you, so we'll be watching you day and night.
Day and night!?
No arguments. You'll stay at Ed's place. He's none too happy about working with gangsters, so you'd better play straight with us.
Okay?
Okay. Besides conversation, what have you got for us, Mr. Collins?

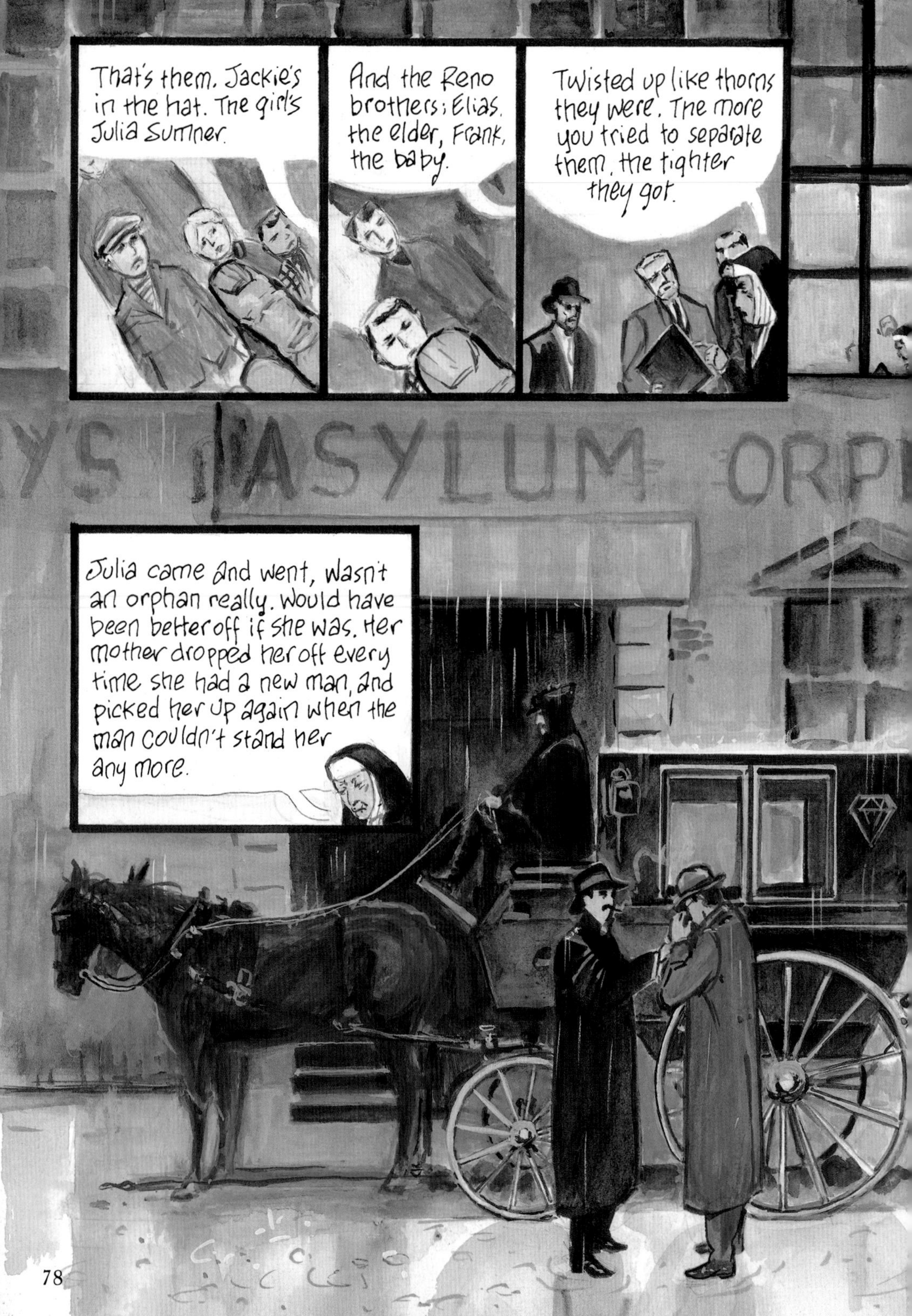
That's them. Jackie's in the hat. The girl's Julia Sumner.
And the Reno brothers; Elias, the elder, Frank, the baby.
Twisted up like thorns they were. The more you tried to separate them, the tighter they got.
Y'S ASYLUM ORP
Julia came and went, wasn't an orphan really. Would have been better off if she was. Her mother dropped her off every time she had a new man, and picked her up again when the man couldn't stand her any more.

The boys; when did they leave?
Just took off one night.

I heard they wound up down in that cesspit on 12th Street and had grown men working for them. No surprise to me.

I heard they all got blown up.

May we borrow the photograph?

Church property. Bring it back.

Why would they wipe out their own gang and blow up the building?

All I could come up with was that Jackie said he was leaving, getting married.
And he went from here to the middle of a corn patch?!

What about the Renos?

They wanted up, not out.

Hardin wouldn't tell me where he was from. He was holding out, sure, but I don't think he knew anything about the bombing.

AW SHIT

When we went to pick him up he was standing at his kid's grave. He turned around in a daze and said "Jules?"

"Jules?"? You said Harte wanted to marry. Marry who?

He never brought her to the bar.

Jules?
Julia?
Julia Sumner?

some clean clothes.
I didn't ask for that.
you're supposed to look like a detective.

Mr. Quindlin said I should hold your gun.
He saw that?
Of course he saw it. It's a detective agency he's running.
Look, I'm-
-You don't pretend to like me. I won't have to pretend you do.

I don't care one way or the other, mister.

SIMMS!
Dwight Emerson's been spotted on the #9 to Grand Central. We gotta move fast!
Me and Larkin been trackin' him from here to Kansas and back and now here he is all dressed and served up.
I'm coming with you.
The Hell you are!

Sorry, I couldn't let him out of my sight but I knew you'd need ME here.
Cletus —
You stay back here, with HIM. Anything goes wrong, get him safely back to the agency.
Cletus Bags. New guy?
Ed, take three men and get all these people out of the way.
Mark, take three guys down the far side of the train. The signal box is holding the other track clear for us.
If we're not careful, this could turn ugly.

256
BALTIMO

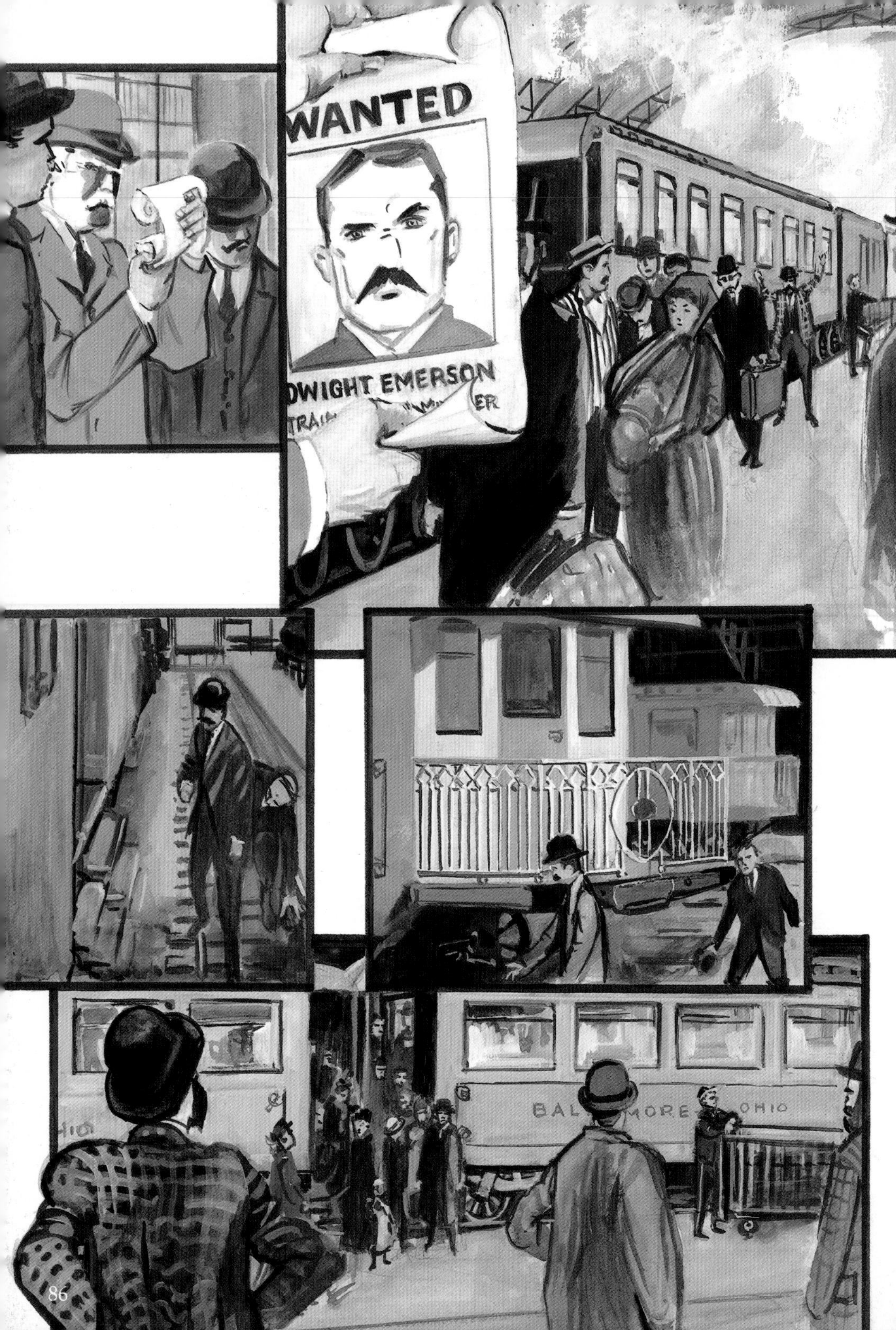
WANTED
DWIGHT EMERSON
BAL MORE-OHIO

Thank-
HEY, WISE GUY!
WHY, I'LL
!?

BLAM
CRASH
CARL! LOOK OUT!
STOP!
Click
Click
DAMN! DAMN!
GEDDOWN! I got it!
BLAM
BLAM

WHAM
DAMN FOOL HADDA PULL HIS GUN OUT!

Dannyboy! Get Carl under the car! I'll cover you.
Ed! there's more of 'em.
BLAM
BLAM

Ed's in the open! give 'im cover!
EVERY BODY DOWN!
MISTER, GET OUTTA THE GODDAM WAY!

Simms, yer damn gun jammed!
Like I said, it's a sign of the times, Billy.
POW POW

I heard you already. Nothing works!!

BAM
BAM
Boss! They're grabbin' people!
Damn! He's been hit!
BAM BAM BAM
BAMBAM
Where's Emerson? Wadda we do?
What we're doin' now: Blast our way out!
Don't hurt my wife, I have money.
His case must be armor-plated. Lucky me!
What the Hell? It's full of cash!
Cletus - follow ten yards behind me.
Now, hold on. You can't go in there. Mr. Quindlin will be hoppin' mad.
It's bedlam.
They've taken that poor woman.
Sounds like the whole Emerson gang showed up.

FUCK!
I say we scrag one of these to show we mean business.
Cletus? I told you to stay back!!

BLAM-AMAM
AM
AM
AM
AM.

Mr. Quindlin: three of our guys hurt, but not bad, seven gangsters shot dead, five of them by "Buffalo Bill" there. Then the pale gent; which column do I put him into?

Good work, Dannyboy.
Doctor Lefarge, This man's so pale he's blue. See if you can get his story. Meanwhile I'll get Buffalo Bill's scalp.

Sadie, we don't need any pictures, except for Collins, and let's put his real name on it.
Oh, oh, Don't look now - it's Secret Service.
Shh.

Carl, create a disturbance for me.

Mr. Quindlin! I see you've recovered Emerson's bank haul. Good work!
Ah. Mr. Phillips.

YOU DUMB CLOWN! Watch where you're going.

Harte, stand very still. I'm going to step forward and take the gun from your belt. No one will see me do it.
Don't get any other ideas or we'll have to let Secret Service handle this, okay?

The whole story's on the table: Larkin's gun, with his name on it, and his badge, both stolen from him in Lebanon by Hardin, the bomber.
But then the doctor in Lebanon says Hardin helped carry in the injured. Mysterious.
He turns up in Chicago, searching for his wife... 'the lady in the watch.'
He comes in here pretending to be a Mr. Collins, but now we know different. Word on the 12th Street gang was that Frank Reno was the brains, Elias, the safecracker, and Harte was the shooter.
Larkin
LARKIN
BLACK DIAMOND
Dear Jackie
Dear Frank
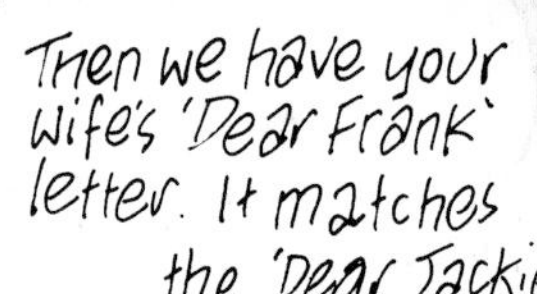

Then we have your wife's 'Dear Frank' letter. It matches the 'Dear Jackie' one.

Mister, I'd say your missis has sold you down the river.

Maybe, but she's not well. She never would'a done it if—
Come on! She wrote Reno an' took off with him.
You don't know a goddamn thing about a goddamn thing.

I said she's not well, and she's not safe, and nothing else matters.
Sweet Christ!

It's all about HER for you, isn't it!!

You were right to wear the glasses. I got your eyes.

It was you who drew the poster?

uh huh.

How?

I listened to people.

That's it?

Will you draw one for me?

Frank Reno.

I'll talk, you draw.

This could be a break if it works. Ed, I want you to stay with him day and night. I can't tell you to go along with this...

He is the accused in the eyes of the law, but we'd never solve this case with him locked up.

Make up your own mind, Ed, but no one else is to know it's Harte we've got, especially not Larkin or Simms.

Okay. You're minding the store. I got an appointment with Secret Service.

Shhsh.

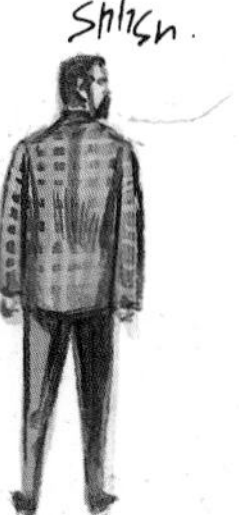

Mr. Phillips has brought me up to date on your fracas at Grand Central. Bravo! An excellent result.
Thank you, Mr. Lambert.
In fact, Mr. Quindlin, we recovered the entirety of a recent robbery perpetrated by the Emerson gang.
Well, all of it except a one hundred dollar bank note.
Maybe they had to make change for carfare.
HA! Maybe so.
I heard about your new man. Quite an addition to your team.
Mr. Collins transferred to us from a rival on the West Coast.
They're All hooligans out there.
Is he settling in well here in the Windy City?
Yes. He's staying with one of my boys until he gets comfortable.

Collins had dealings with our prime suspect once and felt he could be of some value to us.
I guess he'd be the one who led you to the orphanage. That Sister Teresa's a tough customer, eh?
You're right on our heels, I see.
If you kept us posted more thoroughly, Mr. Quindlin, perhaps we could avoid both of us covering the same ground.
But you're doing an excellent job. And speaking of Hardin, what a marvellous portrait you came out with. That's quite an artist you have.
Yes. I'm very proud of her.
Her?
I expect to have the elusive Frank Reno on paper by this time tomorrow.

It doesn't fit together. Lambert says the money was Emerson's haul, but it was the pale guy who was holding it.
And he didn't get off the train with the gang.

He was already there waiting for it to arrive.

I just got back from the morgue. The pale man's name was Grissom.

A swindler who dropped out of police sight a year ago, he looks like he hasn't seen sunlight at least since then.
There was mud on his boots that he didn't pick up anywhere near the rail station.

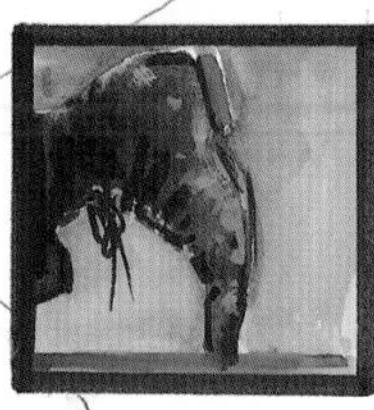
I'll be running tests on this — Back to you, Mr. Quindlin.

Thank you, Doctor Lefarge. Now- what was Secret Service doing at the station anyway?
This business was unrelated to the Lebanon business...
or WAS it?

Pass this bill around.

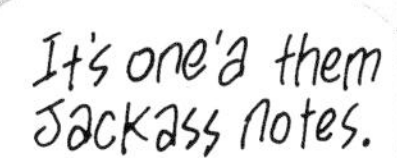
It's one'a them Jackass notes.

Look at the eagle. You turn it upside down, now it's a donkey.
What'll they think of next?

It's a perfectly ordinary $100 bill except the Treasury Department didn't print it.

looked right to me.

Mr. Quindlin wrote the manual on the subject for the Secret Service Treasury Unit. If he says, it's bogus.

What makes that bill ordinary is that it is printed on extraordinary paper. A one-of-a-kind paper.
I'm speculating now but my bet is that the paper was on a sequence of connecting trains, bound for Washington.

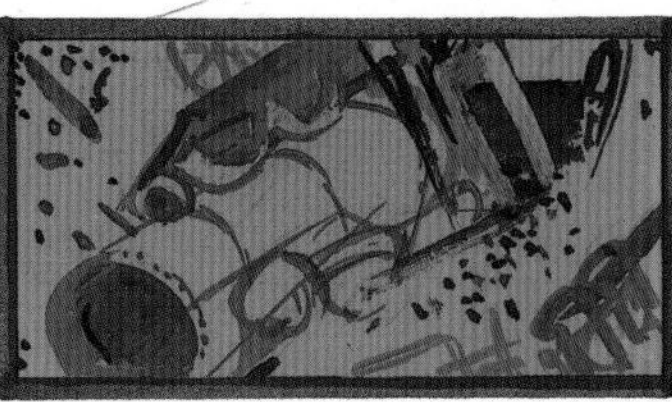
It never got there.

All that destruction, all those people dead...
Just for paper?

A very large amount of it. Enough to screw up the national economy. Or at least, enough to knock over the first domino. Panic would do the rest.

It's a sign of the times. Even money don't work any more.
So we've got Grissom waiting at Grand Central with a bag full of bad money–
Emerson gets off the train with his cronies. Carl sees through his false beard then—
Carl wallops Rattlesnake Jim with his own bag, and notices it's empty!
Now, those two bags were just about identical.
Some kind of swap?

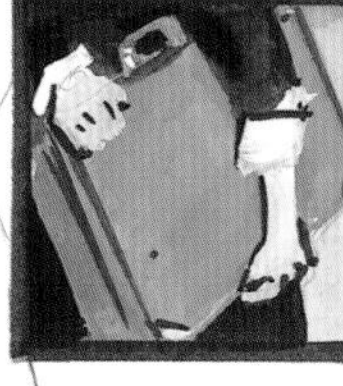

Mr. Collins, were the Renos ever involved in counterfeit?
Never printed any, but the gang moved a big load of bad money once.
Moved it how?

Through small town banks. You go in, clean out the bank, take all the money the town's got, then you leave 'em the bad stuff.
The Hell you say!

You tell 'em if they call the sheriff that the government'll come and take the bad money and the town'll be left dead broke.

It's happened.

or they can spend the money you leave 'em like it's real and maybe by the time it's gone, nobody'll know the diff.

Outta 20 banks, nobody told nobody.

Mr. Collins knows more than an honest man oughtta know.

This is stupid anyway. The Renos and the Emerson gang aren't intelligent enough to work together.

And gangsters are leeches who thrive on a healthy economy. They wouldn't be out to damage it.

What if there's somebody bigger behind it all? And as though he were playing a game of chess, he uses one piece to take the next piece, until the board is cleared.

Checkmate.

Then he would put on his coat and go home.

Then we'd be talking about a foreign agency.

Espionage.

And that's out of our league.

We'll go as far as the Renos and then hand it all over to Secret Service.

Frank Reno! yup. That's him all right.
I'll tidy it up for engraving and get it to the boss first thing tomorrow.
He can decide just how he 'WANTS' mr. Reno.
It's turned cold.
I'd say the snow's coming.
We can walk to my lodgings from here.

BLAM
What you doing under there, Collins? Scared I was going to go for you?
who knows?
I don't like you, Harte, but when I take you down it'll be face to face.
Don't touch a thing. I'll send for the doctor.
Dr. Lefarge, that is.
I've got a messenger in the next building –

He'd have found it harder to get in if 'Sporting Life' here didn't need the damn window open in the middle of December.
He's pale the same as Grissom, and I'm looking at his boot: Sure enough, he's got traces of the same distinctive grey mud.
And he was well briefed. Ed said he went straight for the pillow with the blond mop on it instead of Ed's black hair.
The trouble is, only me, Sadie and Ed ...and the doctor now, know that Harte's here. What about Larkin and Simms? Do you—
Nah, if they figured it out they'd shout their heads off, and they'd be entitled, but not this —
No, wait! I'm getting a bad feeling. I told Lambert that Collins was here.
Oh, Jesus, no! SADIE!
Harte! Wait! — he's unarmed.
I'm right behind him, boss!

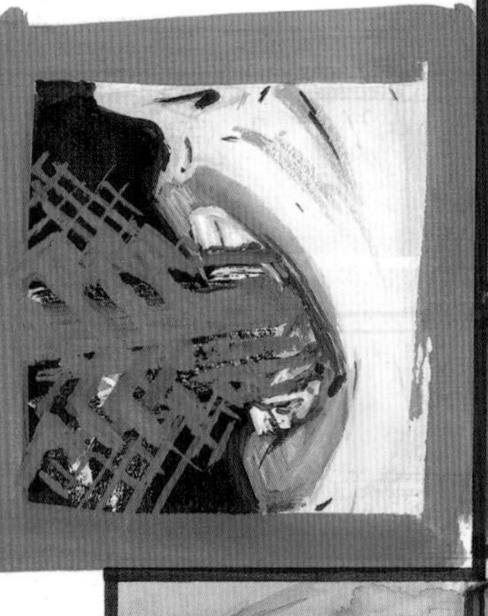

A man in a black coat ran out of Miss Goff's apartment right after she screamed. I didn't know she was out on the ledge.
Dear Lord, when I think about that-
All's well now. Thanks for your alertness, sir, and to your good lady for her help too.

Ed, we're moving fast from here on in. I want Cletus Bags up here to stand guard.

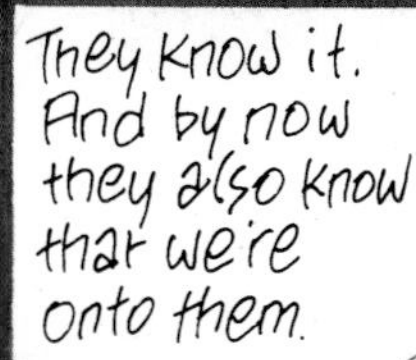
Sadie drew Reno once and she can do it again.
They know it. And by now they also know that we're onto them.
But do WE know who THEY ARE?

I told Lambert and Phillips that 'Collins' was with you in the same breath I told them Sadie was drawing Frank Reno. Big coincidence? I want you to round up the men. Every single one of them.

It's the same mud.

chemical analysis proves it. And I found traces on both Grissom and the man who came through Ed's window after Collins.

It's mud. It could come from anywhere. We're all neck-deep in it this time of year. Mud and horseshit.

Not this mud. It comes from below ground.
..And any other kind of shit.
Like a mine?

But not a mine. It's Chicago River mud. Very old, actually.

But you said its from under ground.
And whats under water?

What you're looking at, gentlemen, is a series of tunnels that were supposed to be an underground railway one day.
The idea was to move merchandise and people and have entry to stores and hotels from below.
You can tunnel under the city and nobody know it?

Believe it or not, it was supposedly being done without the city's knowledge.

I said 'supposedly'. Pay the right people, you can.

What's important is, there was a cave-in last year and men were killed.

The family of one of the victims asked us to investigate. That's how we know about it.

We? I never heard anything. You'd think it woulda made front page.

The city asked us to keep it quiet so they could run their own inquiry.

Ed led our investigation. He'll take it from here.
The tunnel starts in a coal yard...

They used the coal hills as a cover so nobody could see them digging.

Larkin, Simms, you two guard the entrance. Whistle if there's trouble coming down.
Carl- you scout ahead. you'll be quieter than this pack of hooligans.
Light up!
If I remember right, this levels out just ahead then runs for about half a mile before forking three ways. If there's a secret chamber, let's hope it comes before we have to split up –
Hey, Billy, do I see a boat pulling into the landing dock?
If the boss is right that they have to pack up in a hurry, then that old scow's arriving right on time.
Sure doesn't look good for me and you, though.

There's the doc's blue-grey clay.

This sure reminds me what was good about life on the farm.
The wide open spaces, eh? This goes right, you could be back in time for Christmas, Collins.

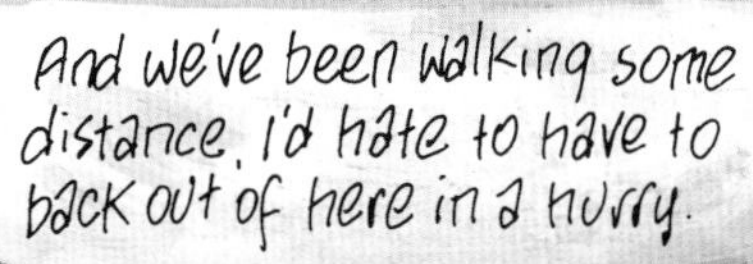
And we've been walking some distance. I'd hate to have to back out of here in a hurry.

Shh - metal shutters... some kind of loading station.
This has to be IT.

WH- GUNFIRE! SHIT!!

Five, six men from the direction of the boat. This is the only thing we can get behind. If they spread out we'll be pegged down.
Hell! They've scattered! Let's just hope time's on our side.
THIS IS THE POLICE! EVERYBODY STAY IN THE OPEN!
BLAM!

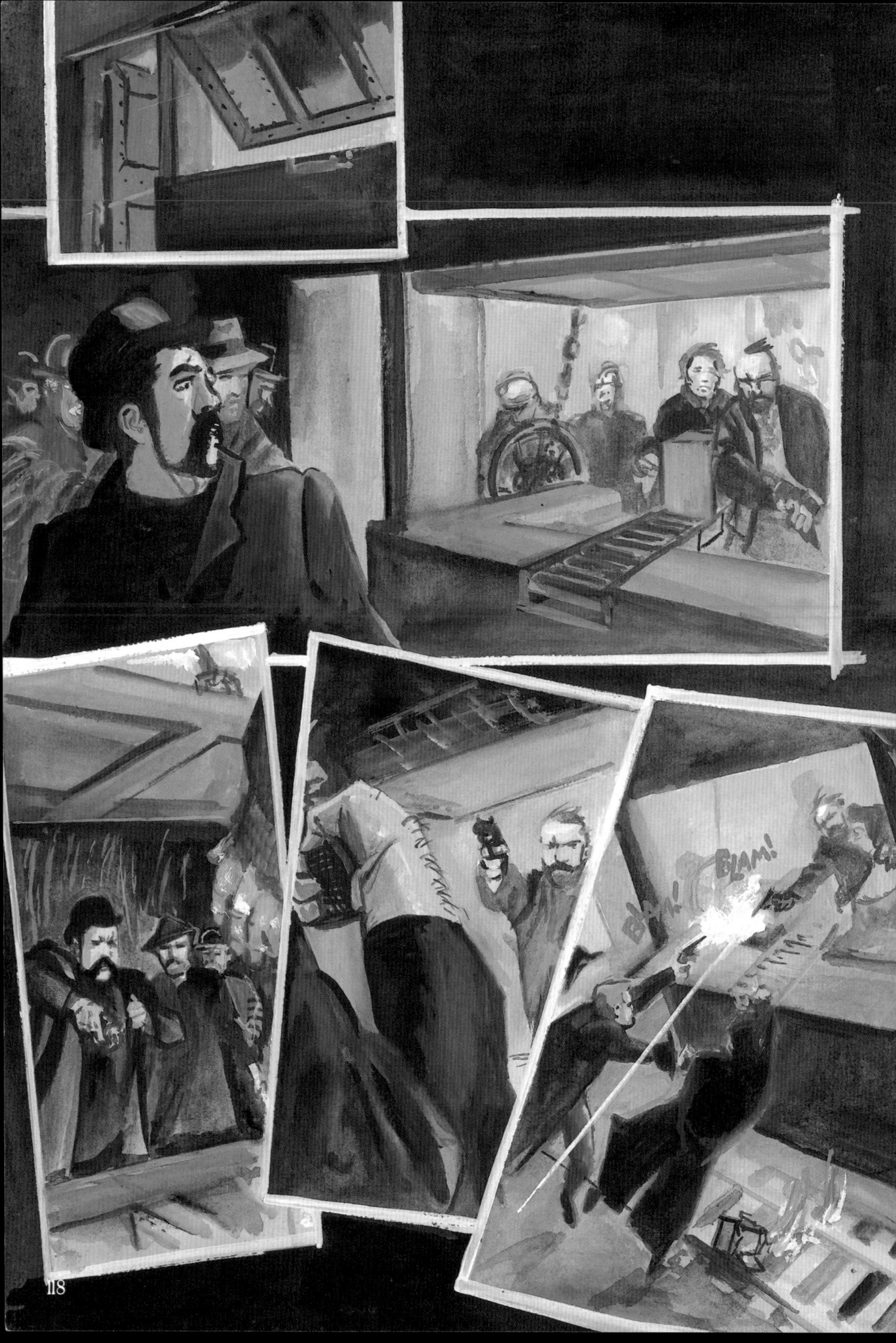
BLAM!

FRANK!

Jackie Harte! So it IS you that's been on our tails.

Where's Jules?
Harte! How many times we got to blow you up?
ELIAS!

Some 'a yer own medicine, Harte!

AW, HELL!

Getting out a back door—can that be—?

Yeh. Phillips!
There's one secret that's out...
...presuming WE get out ourselves.

Everybody out! It's gonna blow!

You're right. Tweety-peeps stopped his singing, but I didn't hear for the uproar.
We won't have time to get all the way back before the gas ignites!
Orderly line, you lowlifes. You'll follow us out –

That noise – a train?

It's Carl!

Everybody in!
What makes this thing go?
It's gotta be one'a them battery operated jobs they been usin' in New York.

This as fast as it goes? Ain't gonna replace the horsey.
fukkinlotswife, don't look back!
Plug yer ears, there's gonna be a big—

BANG

BLAM
BLAM

Looks like the deal's off, boys.

:: cough! :: Dannyboy! Everybody get out?

All of us, none of the counterfeiters!

Simms and Buck are bleeding, Charlie's caught under an ore car and - shit! - Looks like we've lost Ed.

Block their exit, Joe!
Drop the reins, buddy! trip's off!
Inside, mister. you lead.
Eyes front!
My, my, you're leaving in an awful hurry, Lambert.
Quindlin. Well, who would have thought?

But I know EXACTLY who he is.

Ah, Robinson, the charade is over. release the woman.

I never meant to hurt you, Jackie. I just needed to get away.

Every time I looked at you, I saw HER.
Lambert - You were trying to get away yourself before we got here.
ssh- don't-
It's not you... oh, Quindlin, the thought of you 'getting here' never entered my mind.
I don't have a lot of time.
Why, you got a train to catch?
Is that an attempt at humor?
What do you think?
Quindlin, I'll tell you more than you can handle. Out of sour grapes if you like.
What's THAT mean?
You'll see soon enough.
We only brought your agency in for the sake of appearances. If we'd thought-
That "WE" raises a question. Obviously you don't mean the Secret Service. At least, not ours.
"WE" are a consortium of powerful and wealthy men who have been observing the rapid growth of the U.S.A. with much alarm.

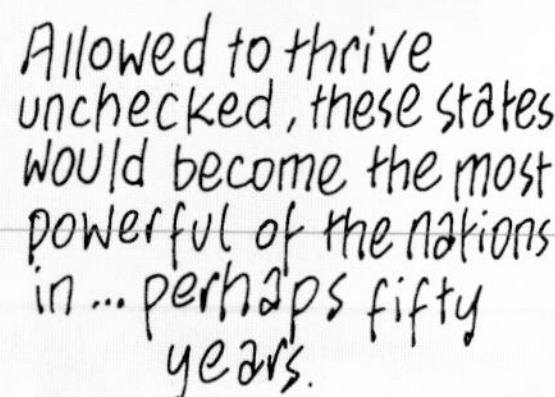
Allowed to thrive unchecked, these states would become the most powerful of the nations in... perhaps fifty years.

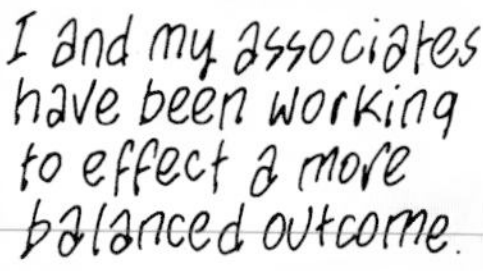
I and my associates have been working to effect a more balanced outcome.

From Europe?
Of course. There's nothing old money loathes more than NEW money.

It may be debated whether the end justified the means.

But then, hired barbarians put the necessary tasks in the hands of other barbarians, their acts emblematic of how these things will be done in the future.
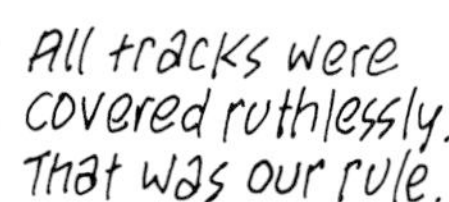
All tracks were covered ruthlessly. That was our rule.

The woman?
That was the Renos' doing. Apparently she presented herself just when they needed a scapegoat. Through her they framed Hardin.
When the scapegoat got out and was running around loose, I had his wife brought here for safe-keeping.

In other words, she might be needed again.
hmm.

I feel a certain regret and I wanted to give the home team a fighting chance before I leave.
Leave? You're going to jail and there's nothing can stop this story getting out–
But WHO would believe it?
Severe damage to the economy of the United States, secretly plotted by the head of one of its own governmental agencies!?
No, I don't think so. People will blame the Jews, like they always do.
But don't concern yourself. There will be other attempts when you and I are gone, in...oh... maybe twenty or thirty years.
Till then, I've given away enough secrets for the man in charge of keeping them.
I'll lead then, shall I? Hardin should keep his head down. There's a low beam–
MR QUINDLIN! WAIT. SOMETHING'S WRO—

Shot in the head! He was expecting it.

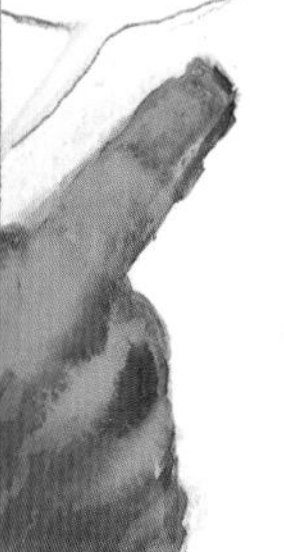

Other side of the park! That red shirt!
It's Phillips!

FAREWELLS

We'll get him, John.
But what'll you do? You'd make a hell of a detective.
Thanks for helping with Jules.
What a story, eh, Bob? You can tell it to your grandkids one day.
But what kind of a story? The hero's an ex-gangster and he's going home with the woman who sold him down the river.
Doesn't sound like any story I ever read. Him and Sadie woulda made a swell couple.

Yes, a publisher offered me a job: a book of photographs showing how the world looks at the turn of the century. I'm going everywhere.
It'll be good to see the world through your eyes, miss.
You'd think the railroad would be quicker.
heh! Yes, that's what I've heard.

It'll be good to get our life back together, Jules.
LLS FARGO

And then the guys in charge turn out to be the villains.
Sign of the times, Billy. My guess is we'll be seeing a lot more of that.
CASTORIA
Quakers
(Toasted)

Electric taxis. Flying buggies. It's all moving too fast for ME, Bob.
You're a nineteenth century man, Billy.
PILSENER BEER ON DRAUGHT
Oh my God! What in blazes is that?
What was that Goddamn noise?
That was the Great Crush Collision March, by Mr. Scott Joplin.
It's about that publicity stunt train crash in Texas, couple'a years back.
I don't get it, Bob - now they're writing music that sounds like a cornfield meet. Next it'll be statues that don't look like nobody and paintings with nothing in 'em but your nightmares.

Don't say it! It's these modern times, eh?
But it truly is, Billy. LOOK! It is now the twentieth century!
Goddamn! It is, too.
Up yours, modern times!!
HA HA.

NEW YORK & LONDON

WWW.FIRSTSECONDBOOKS.COM

Special thanks to Mr. Bill Horberg for his inspired vision.

Published by First Second
First Second is an imprint of Roaring Brook Press, a division of Holtzbrinck Publishing Holdings Limited Partnership
175 Fifth Avenue, New York, NY 10010

Distributed in Canada by H. B. Fenn and Company Ltd.
Distributed in the United Kingdom by Macmillan Children's Books, a division of Pan Macmillan.

Based on the screenplay by C. Gaby Mitchell
Design by Danica Novgorodoff and Charlie Orr

Library of Congress Cataloging-in-Publication Data

Campbell, Eddie, 1955-
The Black Diamond Detective Agency / Eddie Campbell ; based on the screenplay by C. Gaby Mitchell.
p. cm.
ISBN-13: 978-1-59643-142-3
ISBN-10: 1-59643-142-3
1. Graphic novels. I. Mitchell, C. Gaby. II. Title.
PN6727.C29B63 2006
813'.54--dc22
2006050938

COLLECTOR'S EDITION
ISBN-13: 978-1-59643-256-7
ISBN-10: 1-59643-256-X

First Second books are available for special promotions and premiums.
For details, contact: Director of Special Markets, Holtzbrinck Publishers.

First Edition June 2007
Printed in China

10 9 8 7 6 5 4 3 2

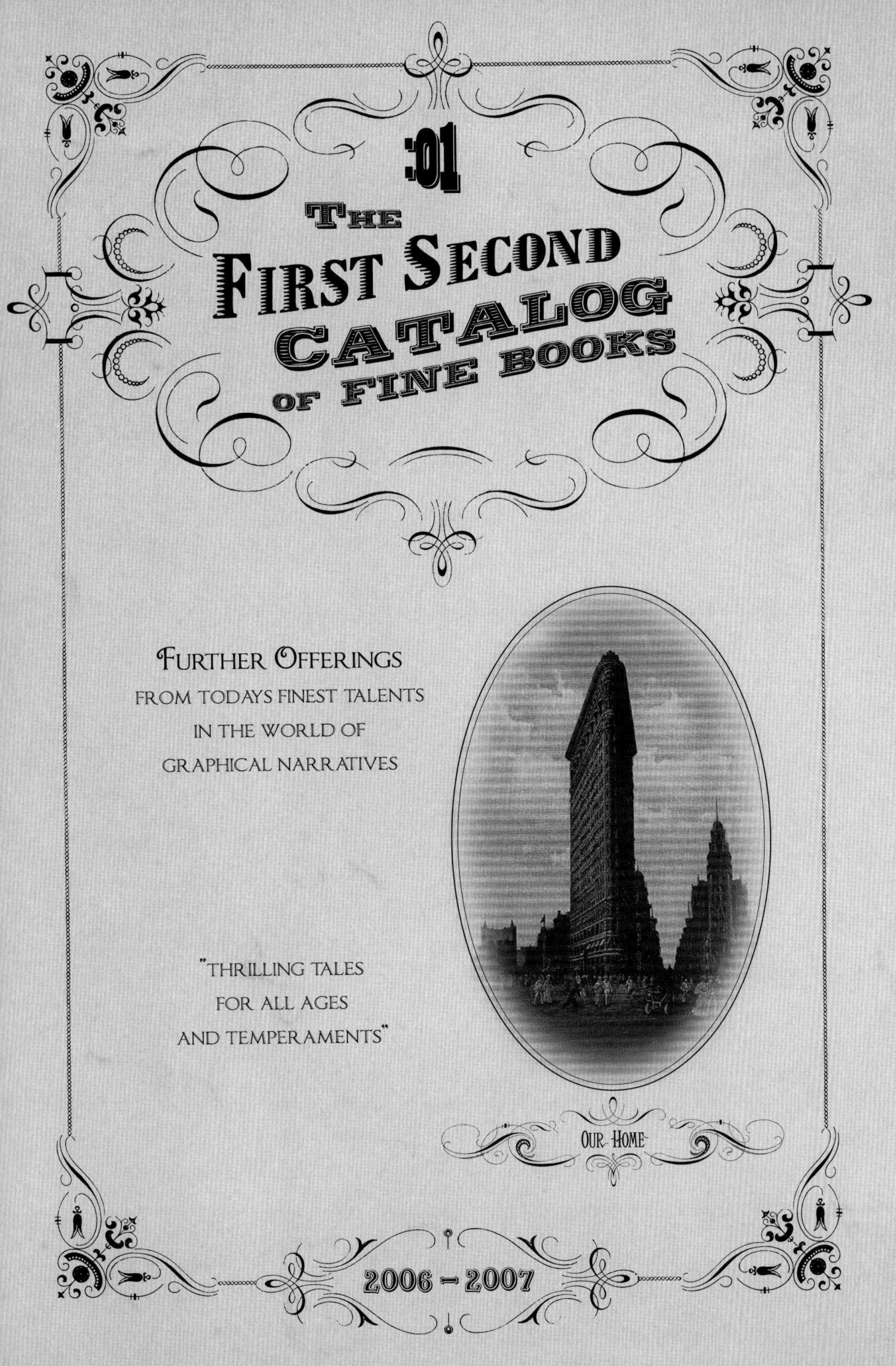
:01
The First Second Catalog of Fine Books
Further Offerings
from todays finest talents
in the world of
graphical narratives
"thrilling tales
for all ages
and temperaments"
Our Home
2006 – 2007

Mr. Campbell's Previous Feat

The Fate of The Artist

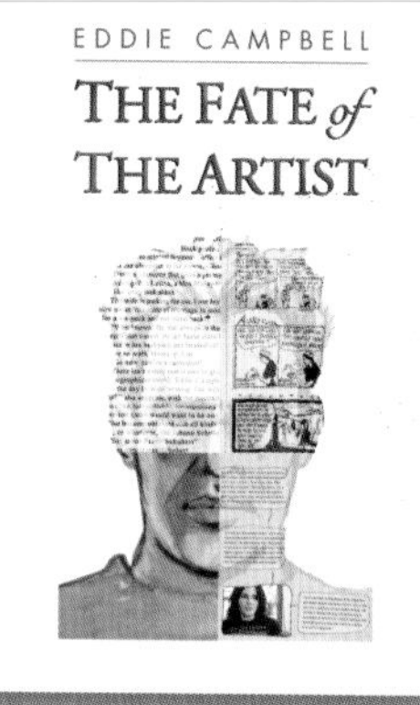

A puzzle, a mystery, and a memoir like no other.

From Mr. Campbell's Advocates

"The Citizen Kane of Graphic Novels"

— Mister Ron's Once A Week

"Playful and wise, Campbell's latest report from the art front continues to demonstrate his mastery of the comics medium."

— ☆ Booklist starred review

"... explodes the genre ... recommended for all adult collections."

—Library Journal

"[a] thoughtful and funny meditation on art and its effect on the artist."

– VOYA

"whimsical and playful...whiplash stylistic shifts from impressionistic caricatures to exquisitely rendered painterly miniatures."

– ☆ Publisher's Weekly starred review

"a dazzling, albeit ambiguously artful experience."

— The Miami Herald

"Not only an autobiographical novel that he calls 'a domestic apocalypse,' but also a meditation on the life of the artist."

— Variety

Other Fine Titles...

A.L.I.E.E.E.N.
by Lewis Trondheim

The first extraterrestrial comic book in print on Planet Earth!

"Like a Pokemon story gone horribly, and hilariously, wrong."

— Publisher's Weekly

The Lost Colony
by Grady Klein

A mysterious island — a boiling concoction of slavery, patriotism, religion, and greed — the story of America itself.

"Chock full of insight."

— VOYA

"[a] witty, sophisticated, candy-colored adventure."

— Booklist

Deogratias **by J.P. Stassen**

The story of a boy caught up in the unthinkable horror of the 1994 Rwandan genocide.

"The importance of the story and the heartbreaking beauty of its presentation make it an essential purchase."

— ☆ Kirkus starred review

"One of the characteristics of all modern genocides is that they exterminate all memories. But in his graphic novel Deogratias, Stassen has successfully created a visual environment of the Tutsi genocide in Rwanda. He ushers us into that unsettling world, and the experience does not leave us unscathed."

— Jean Hatzfeld

Vampire Loves
by Joann Sfar

Love isn't any easier when you're dead.

"Edgy and creepy but at the same time universal and normal, Vampire Loves is a unique study in contrasts that will be a pleasurable discovery for graphic novel enthusiasts."

— VOYA